Uncle Axie's Ugly Tie

Remember what
Uncle Axie says —

"Keep in mind,
  it's easy to be Kind."

Judy Nordstrom
— 2015 —

Uncle Axie's Ugly Tie

JUDY NORDSTROM
Illustrated by Jason Paulhamus

Uncle Axie's Ugly Tie
Published by Judy Nordstrom
Text and Illustrations copyright ©2015 by Judy Nordstrom
Printed in the United States of America

ISBN: 978-1-4909-0412-2

Library of Congress Control Number: 2015905540

Edited by Brenda Judy, www.publishersplanet.com
Cover and Interior Design by Carolyn Sheltraw, www.csheltraw.com
Cover and Interior Illustrations by Jason Paulhamus, www.jasonpaulhamus.com

⊗ This paper meets the requirements of ANSI/NISO Z39.48-1992 (Permanence of Paper).

In memory of Uncle Axie
1920 – 2013

There once was a man from New Jersey called Uncle Axie. He looked a bit peculiar, but he had a heart of gold. If you happened to see him on the street, you might chuckle to yourself and think, "He is a funny looking man."

He always wore a plaid flannel shirt, pants hiked high on his waist, and suspenders to hold them up. He topped off this stylish outfit with a baseball cap and an ugly tie.

Uncle Axie was married to my Aunt Mary. The two of them were always so caring and loving, but never had any children of their own. So, Uncle Axie always helped the neighborhood children; and his motto was, "Keep in mind, it's easy to be kind."

I remember one summer when they took me to the boardwalk to see a band. Uncle Axie carried me high on his shoulders for two hours so I could see the band over the crowd. I asked Uncle Axie how he could hold me up for so long and he said, "Keep in mind, it's easy to be kind."

Every spring Uncle Axie would invite me to his house, and we would color Easter eggs together with special paints and dyes. When I asked Uncle Axie why he was so nice to me, he said, "Keep in mind, it's easy to be kind."

Uncle Axie would always do favors for everyone in his neighborhood; mowing lawns, shoveling snow, and fixing broken pipes. He became the handyman of the neighborhood. Uncle Axie never expected payment or even a "thank you" in return. He often said, "Keep in mind, it's easy to be kind."

Kids in the neighborhood could be mean and make fun of others who were "different"; but Uncle Axie did not let it bother him or stop him from doing good deeds for people. His motto was, "Keep in mind, it's easy to be kind."

Uncle Axie was famous for fixing up old bikes that he found at yard sales. After a fresh coat of spray paint and some new tires, he would give the bike to a neighborhood kid who didn't own a bike. His motto was, "Keep in mind, it's easy to be kind."

Uncle Axie saved his money all year long in a jar on his dresser labeled "vacation." Since I was their only niece, Uncle Axie and Aunt Mary would take me with them on their summer vacation to the shore. When I thanked Uncle Axie, he would always say, "Keep in mind, it's easy to be kind."

Have you ever heard the saying, "You can't judge a book by its cover"? Well, you can't judge people by the way they look, the way they talk, or the way they dress.

Even though Uncle Axie looked unusual, he had a heart of gold. Having a "heart of gold" doesn't mean your heart is made of gold; it means you are generous, sincere, and friendly.

Uncle Axie was a perfect example of a simple but kind man who looked "kind of funny." He may have been the oddest looking man in town—with his high-water pants, old sneakers, and mismatched tie—but he was the most unselfish person I've ever known.

He gave away almost everything he owned, and did not care about material possessions, clothes, or a fancy house.

In his honor, I just had to share this story about a wonderful man who spent his whole life doing things for others. His kindness and generosity are rare qualities in today's world. He touched many lives.

It might do the world some good if we all had a little more "Axie" in us.

About the Author

 Judy Nordstrom attended Bloomsburg University, earning a Master's Degree in Speech/Language Pathology, and has worked with special needs students for the past thirty-five years. Judy grew up in New Jersey where her Uncle Axie made a lasting impression on her life. She always tries to live by his motto, "It's easy to be kind." Judy lives in Williamsport, Pennsylvania, and has two adult children.

43138009R00020

Made in the USA
Charleston, SC
16 June 2015